Words to Know Before You Read

beanstalk

bury

drifted

measure

shovel

sprouts

square

stew

wheelbarrow

yardstick

www.rourkepublishing.com

Edited by Luana K. Mitten
Illustrated by Bob Reese
Art Direction and Page Layout by Renee Brady

Library of Congress Cataloging-in-Publication Data

Picou, Lin
 Dig Plant Feast / Lin Picou.
    p. cm. -- (Little Birdie Books)
 ISBN 978-1-61741-821-1 (hard cover) (alk. paper)
 ISBN 978-1-61236-025-6 (soft cover)
 Library of Congress Control Number: 2011924698

Rourke Publishing
Printed in the United States of America, North Mankato, Minnesota
060711
060711CL

www.rourkepublishing.com - rourke@rourkepublishing.com
Post Office Box 643328 Vero Beach, Florida 32964

Dig, Plant, FEAST!

By Lin Picou

Illustrated by Bob Reese

"Let's plant our friendship garden today." said Ms. Green.

"We'll need the hand shovels put into our wheelbarrow."

"Don't forget your seeds!" reminded Ms. Green as they lined up to go outside.

On the playground, the students discovered a square of dirt. Ms. Green asked each student to dig a small hole then bury a few seeds inside.

"Now we will water your seeds and let the Sun work its magic," said Ms. Green. Using a hose, she made sure the dirt was wet before everyone went back inside.

Weeks later, sprouts came up. Then flowers opened.

"Look!" Carson shouted. "My bean seeds are growing beanstalks!"

"Will we be able to climb the beanstalks?" Cassie asked. Everyone wondered how tall the beanstalks would grow.

13

Ms. Green gave Carson a yardstick so he could measure how much his beanstalks grew every day.

When the flowers turned into long green beans, everyone helped Carson pick them.

The students all agreed to put their vegetables together to make a friendship stew in a big pot.

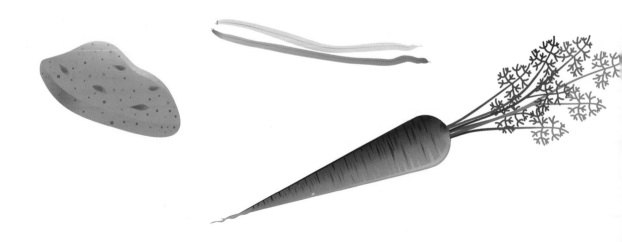

After washing and cutting up carrots, tomatoes, potatoes, and Carson's beans, they cooked the stew with water, salt, and pepper.

The good smells drifted into Mrs. Rose's classroom, so Ms. Green invited them to share their feast. Ms. Green remarked, "Friends shared their seeds and then made new friends by sharing their stew!"

After Reading Activities

You and the Story...

Who planted the friendship garden?

What did they plant in the friendship garden?

What would you plant in a friendship garden?

Tell a friend what you would like to plant in the friendship garden.

Words You Know Now...

Lot's of words have other words hidden in them. Write the words listed below on a sheet of paper. Then circle the small words that you find hiding in the big words.

beanstalk	sprouts
drifted	square
measure	wheelbarrow
shovel	yardstick

You Could...Plant Your Own Friendship Garden

- Decide where you want to plant your garden, outside or inside? Are you going to plant your garden in pots or in the ground?

- What are you going to plant in your garden?

- Create a list of the things you will need to take care of your garden.

- Create a journal to document the progress of your garden as it grows.

- Plan how you will share your garden with family and friends.

About the Author

Lin Picou teaches in Lutz, Florida. Her students practice following directions and math skills when they make fun foods like Dirt Pudding and Jell-O Aquariums for their snacking pleasure.

About the Illustrator

Bob Reese began his art career at age 17 working for Walt Disney. His projects included the animated feature films Sleeping Beauty, The Sword and the Stone, and Paul Bunyan. He has also worked for Bob Clampett and Hanna Barbera Studios. He resides in Utah and enjoys spending time with his two daughters, five grandchildren, and cat named Venus.

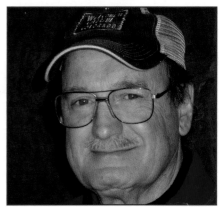